*LITTLE NOVELS BY
        FAVOURITE AUTHORS*

❧ ❧ ❧

Philosophy 4
❧
OWEN WISTER

Owen Wister

Philosophy 4

A Story of Harvard University

BY

OWEN WISTER

AUTHOR OF "THE VIRGINIAN," ETC.

New York
THE MACMILLAN COMPANY
LONDON: MACMILLAN & CO., LTD.
1903

All rights reserved

COPYRIGHT, 1901,
BY THE J. B. LIPPINCOTT COMPANY.

COPYRIGHT, 1903,
BY THE MACMILLAN COMPANY.

Set up and electrotyped April, 1903.

Norwood Press
J. S. Cushing & Co. — Berwick & Smith Co.
Norwood, Mass., U.S.A.

ILLUSTRATIONS

Portrait of Owen Wister . . *Frontispiece*

                                      FACING PAGE

"'Skip Plato,' interrupted one of the Boys" 11

"'Come as near spillin' as you boys wanted, I guess'" 65

I

PHILOSOPHY 4

A STORY OF HARVARD UNIVERSITY

I

TWO frowning boys sat in their tennis flannels beneath the glare of lamp and gas. Their leather belts were loosened, their soft pink shirts unbuttoned at the collar. They were listening with gloomy voracity to the instruction of a third. They sat at a table bared of its customary sporting ornaments, and from time to time they questioned, sucked their pencils, and scrawled vigorous, laconic notes. Their necks and faces shone with the bloom of out-of-doors. Studious concentration was evidently a painful novelty to their features. Drops of perspiration came one by one from their matted hair, and their hands dampened the paper upon which they wrote. The windows stood open wide to the May darkness, but nothing came in save heat and insects; for spring, being behind time, was making up with a sultry burst at the end, as a delayed train makes the last few miles high above schedule speed. Thus it had been since eight o'clock. Eleven was daintily striking now. Its diminutive sonority might have belonged to some church-bell far distant across the Cambridge silence; but it was on a shelf in the room,—a timepiece of Gallic design, representing Mephistopheles, who caressed the world in his lap. And as the little strokes boomed, eight — nine — ten — eleven, the voice of the instructor steadily continued thus: —

"By starting from the Absolute Intelligence, the chief cravings of the reason, after unity and spirituality, receive due satisfaction. Something transcending

"'SKIP PLATO,' INTERRUPTED ONE OF THE BOYS."

the Objective becomes possible. In the *Cogito* the relation of subject and object is implied as the primary condition of all knowledge. Now, Plato never —"

"Skip Plato," interrupted one of the boys. "You gave us his points yesterday."

"Yep," assented the other, rattling through the back pages of his notes. "Got Plato down cold somewhere, — oh, here. He never caught on to the subjective, any more than the other Greek bucks. Go on to the next chappie."

"If you gentlemen have mastered the — the Grreek bucks," observed the instructor, with sleek intonation, "we —"

"Yep," said the second tennis boy, running a rapid judicial eye over his back notes, "you've put us on to their curves enough. Go on."

The instructor turned a few pages forward in the thick book of his own neat type-written notes and then resumed, —

"The self-knowledge of matter in motion."

PHILOSOPHY 4

"Skip it," put in the first tennis boy.

"We went to those lectures ourselves," explained the second, whirling through another dishevelled note-book. "Oh, yes. Hobbes and his gang. There is only one substance, matter, but it doesn't strictly exist. Bodies exist. We've got Hobbes. Go on."

The instructor went forward a few pages more in his exhaustive volume. He had attended all the lectures but three throughout the year, taking them down in short-hand. Laryngitis had kept him from those three, to which, however, he had sent a stenographic friend, so that the chain was unbroken. He now took up the next philosopher on the list; but his smooth discourse was, after a short while, rudely shaken. It was the second tennis boy questioning severely the doctrines imparted.

"So he says color is all your eye, and shape isn't? and substance isn't?"

"Do you mean he claims," said the first boy, equally resentful, "that if we were all extinguished the world would still be here, only there'd be no difference between blue and pink, for instance?"

"The reason is clear," responded the tutor, blandly. He adjusted his eye-glasses, placed their elastic cord behind his ear, and referred to his notes. "It is human sight that distinguishes between colors. If human sight be eliminated from the universe, nothing remains to make the distinction, and consequently there will be none. Thus also is it with sounds. If the universe contains no ear to hear the sound, the sound has no existence."

"Why?" said both the tennis boys at once.

The tutor smiled. "Is it not clear," said he, "that there can be no sound if it is not heard?"

"No," they both returned, "not in the least clear."

"It's clear enough what he's driving at, of course," pursued the first boy. "Until the waves of sound or light or what not hit us through our senses, our brains don't experience the sensations of sound or light or what not, and so, of course, we can't know about them — not until they reach us."

"Precisely," said the tutor. He had a suave and slightly alien accent.

"Well, just tell me how that proves a thunder-storm in a desert island makes no noise."

"If a thing is inaudible — " began the tutor.

"That's mere juggling!" vociferated the boy. "That's merely the same kind of toy-shop brain-trick you gave us out of Greek philosophy yesterday. They said there was no such thing as motion because at every instant of time the moving body had to be somewhere, so how could it get anywhere else? Good Lord! I can make up foolishness like that myself. For instance: A moving body can never stop. Why? Why, because at every instant of time it must be going at a certain rate, so how can it ever get slower? Pooh!" He stopped. He had been gesticulating with one hand, which he now jammed wrathfully into his pocket.

The tutor must have derived great pleasure from his own smile, for he prolonged and deepened and variously modified it, while his shiny little calculating eyes travelled from one to the other of his ruddy scholars. He coughed, consulted his notes, and went through all the paces of superiority. "I can find nothing about a body's being unable to stop," said he, gently. "If logic makes no appeal to you, gentlemen—"

"Oh, bunch!" exclaimed the second tennis boy, in the slang of his period, which was the early eighties. "Look here. Color has no existence outside of our brain—that's the idea?"

The tutor bowed.

"And sound hasn't? and smell hasn't? and taste hasn't?"

The tutor had repeated his little bow after each.

"And that's because they depend on our senses? Very well. But he claims solidity and shape and distance do exist independently of us. If we all died, they'd be here just the same, though the others wouldn't. A flower would go on growing, but it would stop smelling. Very well. Now you tell me how we ascertain solidity. By the touch, don't we? Then, if there was nobody to touch an object, what then? Seems to me touch is just as much of a sense as your nose is." (He meant no personality, but the first boy choked a giggle as the speaker hotly followed up his thought.) "Seems to me by his reasoning that in a desert island there'd be nothing at all — smells or shapes — not even an island. Seems to me that's what you call logic."

The tutor directed his smile at the open window. "Berkeley —" said he.

"By Jove!" said the other boy, not heeding him, "and here's another point: If color is entirely in my brain, why don't that ink-bottle and this shirt look alike to me? They ought to. And why don't a Martini cocktail and a cup of coffee taste the same to my tongue?"

"Berkeley," attempted the tutor, "demonstrates —"

"Do you mean to say," the boy rushed on, "that there is no eternal quality in all these things which when it meets my perceptions compels me to see differences?"

The tutor surveyed his notes. "I can discover no such suggestions here as you are pleased to make," said he. "But your orriginal rresearches," he continued most obsequiously, "recall our next subject, — Berkeley and the Idealists." And he smoothed out his notes.

"Let's see," said the second boy, pondering; "I went to two or three lectures about that time. Berkeley — Berkeley. Didn't he — oh, yes! he did. He went the whole hog. Nothing's anywhere except in your ideas. You think the table's there, but it isn't. There isn't any table."

The first boy slapped his leg and lighted a cigarette. "I remember," said he. "Amounts to this: If I were to stop thinking about you, you'd evaporate."

"Which is balls," observed the second boy, judicially, again in the slang of his period, "and can be proved so. For you're not always thinking about me, and I've never evaporated once."

The first boy, after a slight wink at the second, addressed the tutor. "Supposing you were to happen to forget yourself," said he to that sleek gentleman, "would you evaporate?"

The tutor turned his little eyes doubtfully upon the tennis boys, but answered, reciting the language of his notes: "The idealistic theory does not apply to the thinking ego, but to the world of external phenomena. The world exists in our conception of it."

"Then," said the second boy, "when a thing is inconceivable?"

"It has no existence," replied the tutor, complacently.

"But a billion dollars is inconceivable," retorted the boy. "No mind can take in a sum of that size; but it exists."

"Put that down! put that down!" shrieked the other boy. "You've struck something. If we get Berkeley on the paper, I'll run that in." He wrote rapidly, and then took a turn around the room, frowning as he walked. "The actuality of a thing," said he, summing his clever thoughts up, "is not disproved by its being inconceivable. Ideas alone depend upon thought for their existence. There! Anybody can get off stuff like that by the yard." He picked up a cork and a foot-rule, tossed the cork, and sent it flying out of the window with the foot-rule.

"Skip Berkeley," said the other boy. "How much more is there?"

"Necessary and accidental truths," answered the tutor, reading the subjects from his notes. "Hume and the causal law. The duality, or multiplicity, of the ego."

"The hard-boiled ego," commented the boy with the ruler; and he batted a swooping June-bug into space.

"Sit down, idiot," said his sprightly mate.

Conversation ceased. Instruction went forward. Their pencils worked. The causal law, etc., went into their condensed notes like Liebig's extract of beef, and drops of perspiration continued to trickle from their matted hair.

II

II

BERTIE and Billy were sophomores. They had been alive for twenty years, and were young. Their tutor was also a sophomore. He too had been alive for twenty years, but never yet had become young. Bertie and Billy had colonial names (Rogers, I think, and Schuyler), but the tutor's name was Oscar Maironi, and he was charging his pupils five dollars an hour each for his instruction. Do not think this excessive. Oscar could have tutored a whole class of irresponsibles, and by that arrangement have earned probably more; but Bertie and Billy had preempted him on account of his fame for high standing and accuracy, and they could well afford it. All three sophomores alike had happened to choose Philosophy 4 as one of their elective courses, and all alike were now face to face with the Day of Judgment. The final examinations had begun. Oscar could lay his hand upon his studious heart and await the Day of Judgment like — I had nearly said a Christian! His notes were full: Three hundred pages about Zeno and Parmenides and the rest, almost every word as it had come from the professor's lips. And his memory was full, too, flowing like a player's lines. With the right cue he could recite instantly: "An important application of this principle, with obvious reference to Heracleitos, occurs in Aristotle, who says —" He could do this with the notes anywhere. I am sure you appreciate Oscar and his great power of acquiring facts. So he was ready, like the wise virgins of parable. Bertie and Billy did not put one in mind of virgins: although they had burned considerable midnight oil, it had not been to throw light upon Philosophy 4. In them the mere word Heracleitos had raised a chill no later than yesterday,— the chill of the unknown. They had not attended the lectures on the "Greek bucks." Indeed, profiting by their privilege of voluntary recitations, they had dropped in but seldom on Philosophy 4. These blithe grasshoppers had danced and sung away the precious storing season, and now that the bleak hour of examinations was upon them, their waked-up hearts had felt aghast at the sudden vision of their ignorance. It was on a Monday noon that this feeling came fully upon them, as they read over the names of the philosophers. Thursday was the day of the examination. "Who's Anaxagoras?" Billy had inquired of Bertie. "I'll tell you," said Bertie, "if you'll tell me who Epicharmos of Kos was." And upon this they embraced with helpless laughter. Then they reckoned up the hours left for them to learn Epicharmos of Kos in, — between Monday noon and Thursday morning at nine, — and their quailing chill increased. A tutor must be called in at once. So the grasshoppers, having money, sought out and quickly purchased the ant.

Closeted with Oscar and his notes, they had, as Bertie put it, salted down the early Greek bucks by seven on Monday evening. By the same midnight they had, as Billy expressed it, called the turn on Plato. Tuesday was a second day of concentrated swallowing. Oscar had taken them through the thought of many centuries. There had been intermissions for lunch and dinner only; and the weather was exceedingly hot. The pale-skinned Oscar stood this strain better than the unaccustomed Bertie and Billy. Their jovial eyes had grown hollow to-night, although their minds were going gallantly, as you have probably noticed. Their criticisms, slangy and abrupt, struck the scholastic

Oscar as flippancies which he must indulge, since the pay was handsome. That these idlers should jump in with doubts and questions not contained in his sacred notes raised in him feelings betrayed just once in that remark about "orriginal rresearch."

"Nine — ten — eleven — twelve," went the little timepiece; and Oscar rose.

"Gentlemen," he said, closing the sacred notes, "we have finished the causal law."

"That's the whole business except the ego racket, isn't it?" said Billy.

"The duality, or multiplicity, of the ego remains," Oscar replied.

"Oh, I know its name. It ought to be a soft snap after what we've had."

"Unless it's full of dates and names you've got to know," said Bertie.

"Don't believe it is," Billy answered. "I heard him at it once." (This meant that Billy had gone to a lecture lately.) "It's all about Who am I? and How do I do it?" Billy added.

"Hm!" said Bertie. "Hm! Subjective and objective again, I suppose, only applied to oneself. You see, that table is objective. I can stand off and judge it. It's outside of me; has nothing to do with me. That's easy. But my opinion of — well, my — well, anything in my nature — "

"Anger when it's time to get up," suggested Billy.

"An excellent illustration," said Bertie. "That is subjective in me. Similar to your dislike of water as a beverage. That is subjective in you. But here comes the twist. I can think of my own anger and judge it, just as if it were an outside thing, like a table. I can compare it with itself on different mornings or with other people's anger. And I trust that you can do the same with your thirst."

"Yes," said Billy; "I recognize that it is greater at times and less at others."

"Very well. There you are. Duality of the ego."

"Subject and object," said Billy. "Perfectly true, and very queer when you try to think of it. Wonder how far it goes? Of course, one can explain the body's being an object to the brain inside it. That's mind and matter over again. But when my own mind and thought can become objects to themselves — I wonder how far that does go?" he broke off musingly. "What useless stuff!" he ended.

"Gentlemen," said Oscar, who had been listening to them with patient, Oriental diversion, "I —"

"Oh," said Bertie, remembering him. "Look here. We mustn't keep you up. We're awfully obliged for the way you are putting us on to this. You're saving our lives. Ten to-morrow for a grand review of the whole course."

"And the multiplicity of the ego?" inquired Oscar.

"Oh, I forgot. Well, it's too late to-night. Is it much? Are there many dates and names and things?"

"It is more of a general inquiry and analysis," replied Oscar. "But it is forty pages of my notes." And he smiled.

"Well, look here. It would be nice to have to-morrow clear for review. We're not tired. You leave us your notes and go to bed."

Oscar's hand almost moved to cover and hold his precious property, for this instinct was the deepest in him. But it did not so move, because his intelligence controlled his instinct nearly, though not quite, always. His shiny little eyes, however, became furtive and antagonistic — something the boys did not at first make out.

Oscar gave himself a moment of silence. "I could not brreak my rule," said he then. "I do not ever leave my notes with anybody. Mr. Woodridge asked for my History 3 notes, and Mr. Bailey wanted my notes for Fine Arts 1, and I could not let them have them. If Mr. Woodridge was to hear — "

"But what in the dickens are you afraid of?"

"Well, gentlemen, I would rather not. You would take good care, I know, but there are sometimes things which happen that we cannot help. One time a fire—"

At this racial suggestion both boys made the room joyous with mirth. Oscar stood uneasily contemplating them. He would never be able to understand them, not as long as he lived, nor they him. When their mirth was over he did somewhat better, but it was tardy. You see, he was not a specimen of the first rank, or he would have said at once what he said now: "I wish to study my notes a little myself, gentlemen."

"Go along, Oscar, with your inflammable notes, go along!" said Bertie, in supreme good-humor. "And we'll meet to-morrow at ten—if there hasn't been a fire. Better keep your notes in the bath, Oscar."

In as much haste as could be made with a good appearance, Oscar buckled his volume in its leather cover, gathered his hat and pencil, and, bidding his pupils a very good night, sped smoothly out of the room.

III

III

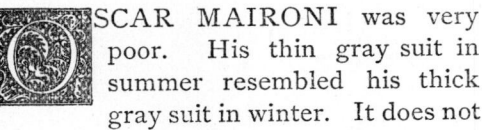

OSCAR MAIRONI was very poor. His thin gray suit in summer resembled his thick gray suit in winter. It does not seem that he had more than two; but he had a black coat and waistcoat, and a narrow-brimmed, shiny hat to go with these, and one pair of patent-leather shoes that laced, and whose long soles curved upward at the toe like the rockers of a summer-hotel chair. These holiday garments served him in all seasons; and when you saw him dressed in them, and seated in a car bound for Park Square, you knew he was going into Boston, where he would read manuscript essays on Botticelli or Pico della Mirandola, or manuscript translations of Armenian folk-songs; read these to ecstatic, dim-eyed ladies in Newbury

Street, who would pour him cups of tea when it was over, and speak of his earnestness after he was gone. It did not do the ladies any harm; but I am not sure that it was the best thing for Oscar. It helped him feel every day, as he stepped along to recitations with his elbow clamping his books against his ribs and his heavy black curls bulging down from his gray slouch hat to his collar, how meritorious he was compared with Bertie and Billy — with all Berties and Billies. He may have been. Who shall say? But I will say at once that chewing the cud of one's own virtue gives a sour stomach.

Bertie's and Billy's parents owned town and country houses in New York. The parents of Oscar had come over in the steerage. Money filled the pockets of Bertie and Billy; therefore were their heads empty of money and full of less cramping thoughts. Oscar had fallen upon the reverse of this fate. Calculation was his second nature. He had given his education to himself; he had for its sake toiled, traded, outwitted, and saved. He had sent himself to college, where most of the hours not given to education and more education, went to toiling and more toiling, that he might pay his meagre way through the college world. He had a cheaper room and ate cheaper meals than was necessary. He tutored, and he wrote college specials for several newspapers. His chief relaxation was the praise of the ladies in Newbury Street. These told him of the future which awaited him, and when they gazed upon his features were put in mind of the dying Keats. Not that Oscar was going to die in the least. Life burned strong in him. There were sly times when he took what he had saved by his cheap meals and room and went to Boston with it, and for a few hours thoroughly ceased being ascetic. Yet Oscar felt meritorious when he considered Bertie and Billy; for, like the socialists, merit with him meant not being able to live as well as your neighbor. You will think that I have given to Oscar what is familiarly termed a black eye. But I was once inclined to applaud his struggle for knowledge, until I studied him close and perceived that his love was not for the education he was getting. Bertie and Billy loved play for play's own sake, and in play forgot themselves, like the wholesome young creatures that they were. Oscar had one love only : through all his days whatever he might forget, he would remember himself ; through all his days he would make knowledge show that self off. Thank heaven, all the poor students in Harvard College were not Oscars ! I loved some of them as much as I loved Bertie and Billy. So there is no black eye about it. Pity Oscar, if you like ; but don't be so mushy as to admire him as he stepped along in the night, holding his notes, full of his knowledge, thinking of Bertie and Billy, conscious of virtue, and smiling his smile.

They were not conscious of any virtue, were Bertie and Billy, nor were they smiling. They were solemnly eating up together a box of handsome strawberries and sucking the juice from their reddened thumbs.

"Rather mean not to make him wait and have some of these after his hard work on us," said Bertie. "I'd forgotten about them."

"He ran out before you could remember, anyway," said Billy.

"Wasn't he absurd about his old notes?" Bertie went on, a new strawberry in his mouth. "We don't need them, though. With to-morrow we'll get this course down cold."

"Yes, to-morrow," sighed Billy. "It's awful to think of another day of this kind."

"Horrible," assented Bertie.

"He knows a lot. He's extraordinary," said Billy.

"Yes, he is. He can talk the actual words of the notes. Probably he could teach the course himself. I don't suppose he buys any strawberries, even when they get ripe and cheap here. What's the matter with you?"

Billy had broken suddenly into merriment. "I don't believe Oscar owns a bath," he explained.

"By Jove! so his notes will burn in spite of everything!" And both of the tennis boys shrieked foolishly.

Then Billy began taking his clothes off, strewing them in the window-seat, or anywhere that they happened to drop; and Bertie, after hitting another cork or two out of the window with the tennis racket, departed to his own room on another floor and left Billy to immediate and deep slumber. This was broken for a few moments when Billy's room-mate returned happy from an excursion which had begun in the morning.

The room-mate sat on Billy's feet until that gentleman showed consciousness.

"I've done it," said the room-mate, then.

"The hell you have!"

"You couldn't do it."

"The hell I couldn't!"

"Great dinner."

"The hell it was!"

"Soft-shell crabs, broiled live lobster, salmon, grass-plover, dough-birds, rum omelette. Bet you five dollars you can't find it."

"Take you. Go to bed." And Billy fell again into deep, immediate slumber.

The room-mate went out into the sitting room, and noting the signs there of the hard work which had gone on during his absence, was glad that he did not take Philosophy 4. He was soon asleep also.

IV

IV

BILLY got up early. As he plunged into his cold bath he envied his room-mate, who could remain at rest indefinitely, while his own hard lot was hurrying him to prayers and breakfast and Oscar's inexorable notes. He sighed once more as he looked at the beauty of the new morning and felt its air upon his cheeks. He and Bertie belonged to the same club-table, and they met there mournfully over the oatmeal. This very hour to-morrow would see them eating their last before the examination in Philosophy 4. And nothing pleasant was going to happen between,—nothing that they could dwell upon with the slightest satisfaction. Nor had their sleep entirely refreshed them. Their eyes were not quite right, and their hair, though it was brushed, showed fatigue of the nerves in a certain inclination to limpness and disorder.

> "Epicharmos of Kos
> Was covered with moss,"

remarked Billy.

> "Thales and Zeno
> Were duffers at keno,"

added Bertie.

In the hours of trial they would often express their education thus.

"Philosophers I have met," murmured Billy, with scorn. And they ate silently for some time.

"There's one thing that's valuable," said Bertie next. "When they spring those tricks on you about the flying arrow not moving, and all the rest, and prove it all right by logic, you learn what pure logic amounts to when it cuts loose from common sense. And Oscar thinks it's immense. We shocked him."

"He's found the Bird-in-Hand!" cried Billy, quite suddenly.

"Oscar?" said Bertie, with an equal shout.

"No, John. John has. Came home last night and waked me up and told me."

"Good for John," remarked Bertie, pensively.

Now, to the undergraduate mind of that day the Bird-in-Hand tavern was what the golden fleece used to be to the Greeks, — a sort of shining, remote, miraculous thing, difficult though not impossible to find, for which expeditions were fitted out. It was reported to be somewhere in the direction of Quincy, and in one respect it resembled a ghost: you never saw a man who had seen it himself; it was always his cousin, or his elder brother in '79. But for the successful explorer a dinner and wines were waiting at the Bird-in-Hand more delicious than anything outside of Paradise. You will realize, therefore, what a thing it was to have a room-mate who had attained. If Billy had not been so dog-tired last night, he would have sat up and made John tell him everything from beginning to end.

"Soft-shell crabs, broiled live lobster, salmon, grass-plover, dough-birds, and rum omelette," he was now reciting to Bertie.

"They say the rum there is old Jamaica brought in slave-ships," said Bertie, reverently.

"I've heard he has white port of 1820," said Billy; "and claret and champagne."

Bertie looked out of the window. "This is the finest day there's been," said he. Then he looked at his watch. It was twenty-five minutes before Oscar. Then he looked Billy hard in the eye. "Have you any sand?" he inquired.

It was a challenge to Billy's manhood. "Sand!" he yelled, sitting up.

Both of them in an instant had left the table and bounded out of the house.

"I'll meet you at Pike's," said Billy to Bertie. "Make him give us the black gelding."

"Might as well bring our notes along," Bertie called after his rushing friend; "and get John to tell you the road."

To see their haste, as the two fled in opposite directions upon their errands, you would have supposed them under some crying call of obligation, or else to be escaping from justice.

Twenty minutes later they were seated behind the black gelding and bound on their journey in search of the Bird-in-Hand. Their notes in Philosophy 4 were stowed under the buggy-seat.

"Did Oscar see you?" Bertie inquired.

"Not he," cried Billy, joyously.

"Oscar will wonder," said Bertie; and he gave the black gelding a triumphant touch with the whip.

You see, it was Oscar that had made them run so; or, rather, it was Duty and Fate walking in Oscar's displeasing likeness. Nothing easier, nothing more reasonable, than to see the tutor and tell him they should not need him to-day.

But that would have spoiled everything. They did not know it, but deep in their childlike hearts was a delicious sense that in thus unaccountably disappearing they had won a great game, had got away ahead of Duty and Fate. After all, it did bear some resemblance to an escape from justice.

Could he have known this, Oscar would have felt more superior than ever. Punctually at the hour agreed, ten o'clock, he rapped at Billy's door and stood waiting, his leather wallet of notes nipped safe between elbow and ribs. Then he knocked again. Then he tried the door, and as it was open, he walked deferentially into the sitting room. Sonorous snores came from one of the bedrooms. Oscar peered in and saw John; but he saw no Billy in the other bed. Then, always deferential, he sat down in the sitting room and watched a couple of prettily striped coats hanging in a half-open closet.

At that moment the black gelding

was flirtatiously crossing the drawbridge over the Charles on the Allston Road. The gelding knew the clank of those suspending chains and the slight unsteadiness of the meeting halves of the bridge as well as it knew oats. But it could not enjoy its own entirely premeditated surprise quite so much as Bertie and Billy were enjoying their entirely unpremeditated flight from Oscar. The wind rippled on the water; down at the boat-house Smith was helping some one embark in a single scull; they saw the green meadows toward Brighton; their foreheads felt cool and unvexed, and each new minute had the savor of fresh forbidden fruit.

"How do we go?" said Bertie.

"I forgot I had a bet with John until I had waked him," said Billy. "He bet me five last night I couldn't find it, and I took him. Of course, after that I had no right to ask him anything, and he thought I was funny. He said I couldn't find out if the landlady's hair was her own. I went him another five on that."

"How do you say we ought to go?" said Bertie, presently.

"Quincy, I'm sure."

They were now crossing the Albany tracks at Allston. "We're going to get there," said Bertie; and he turned the black gelding toward Brookline and Jamaica Plain.

The enchanting day surrounded them. The suburban houses, even the suburban street-cars, seemed part of one great universal plan of enjoyment. Pleasantness so radiated from the boys' faces and from their general appearance of clean white flannel trousers and soft clean shirts of pink and blue that a driver on a passing car leaned to look after them with a smile and a butcher hailed them with loud brotherhood from his cart. They turned a corner, and from a long way off came the sight of the tower of Memorial Hall. Plain above all intervening tenements and foliage it rose.

Over there beneath its shadow were examinations and Oscar. It caught Billy's roving eye, and he nudged Bertie, pointing silently to it. "Ha, ha!" sang Bertie. And beneath his light whip the gelding sprang forward into its stride.

The clocks of Massachusetts struck eleven. Oscar rose doubtfully from his chair in Billy's study. Again he looked into Billy's bedroom and at the empty bed. Then he went for a moment and watched the still forcibly sleeping John. He turned his eyes this way and that, and after standing for a while moved quietly back to his chair and sat down with the leather wallet of notes on his lap, his knees together, and his unblacked shoes touching. In due time the clocks of Massachusetts struck noon.

In a meadow where a brown amber stream ran, lay Bertie and Billy on the grass. Their summer coats were off, their belts loosened. They watched with eyes half closed the long waterweeds moving gently as the current waved and twined them. The black gelding, brought along a farm road and through a gate, waited at its ease in the field beside a stone wall. Now and then it stretched and cropped a young leaf from a vine that grew over the wall, and now and then the warm wind brought down the fruit blossoms all over the meadow. They fell from the tree where Bertie and Billy lay, and the boys brushed them from their faces. Not very far away was Blue Hill, softly shining; and crows high up in the air came from it occasionally across here.

By one o'clock a change had come in Billy's room. Oscar during that hour had opened his satchel of philosophy upon his lap and read his notes attentively. Being almost word perfect in many parts of them, he now spent his unexpected leisure in acquiring accurately the language of still further paragraphs. "The sharp line of demarcation which Descartes drew between consciousness and the material world," whispered Oscar with satisfaction, and knew that if Descartes were on the examination paper he could start with this and go on for nearly twenty lines before he would have to use any words of his own. As he memorized, the chambermaid, who had come to do the bedrooms three times already and had gone away again, now returned and no longer restrained her indignation. "Get up, Mr. Blake!" she vociferated to the sleeping John; "you ought to be ashamed!" And she shook the bedstead. Thus John had come to rise and discover Oscar. The patient tutor explained himself as John listened in his pyjamas.

"Why, I'm sorry," said he, "but I don't believe they'll get back very soon."

"They have gone away?" asked Oscar, sharply.

"Ah — yes," returned the reticent John. "An unexpected matter of importance."

"But, my dear sir, those gentlemen know nothing! Philosophy 4 is to-morrow, and they know nothing."

"They'll have to stand it, then," said John, with a grin.

"And my time. I am waiting here. I am engaged to teach them. I have been waiting here since ten. They engaged me all day and this evening."

"I don't believe there's the slightest use in your waiting now, you know. They'll probably let you know when they come back."

"Probably! But they have engaged my time. The girl knows I was here ready at ten. I call you to witness that you found me waiting, ready at any time."

John in his pyjamas stared at Oscar. "Why, of course they'll pay you the whole thing," said he, coldly; "stay here

PHILOSOPHY 4

if you prefer." And he went into the bathroom and closed the door.

The tutor stood awhile, holding his notes and turning his little eyes this way and that. His young days had been dedicated to getting the better of his neighbor, because otherwise his neighbor would get the better of him. Oscar had never suspected the existence of boys like John and Bertie and Billy. He stood holding his notes, and then, buckling them up once more, he left the room with evidently reluctant steps. It was at this time that the clocks struck one.

In their field among the soft new grass sat Bertie and Billy some ten yards apart, each with his back against an apple tree. Each had his notes and took his turn at questioning the other. Thus the names of the Greek philosophers with their dates and doctrines were shouted gayly in the meadow. The foreheads of the boys were damp to-day, as they had been last night, and their shirts were opened to the air; but it was the sun that made them hot now, and no lamp or gas; and already they looked twice as alive as they had looked at breakfast. There they sat, while their memories gripped the summarized list of facts essential, facts to be known accurately; the simple, solid, raw facts, which, should they happen to come on the examination paper, no skill could evade nor any imagination supply. But this study was no longer dry and dreadful to them: they had turned it to a sporting event. "What about Heracleitos?" Billy as catechist would put at Bertie. "Eternal flux," Bertie would correctly snap back at Billy. Or, if he got it mixed up, and replied, "Everything is water," which was the doctrine of another Greek, then Billy would credit himself with twenty-five cents on a piece of paper. Each ran a memorandum of this kind; and you can readily see how spirited a character metaphysics would assume under such conditions.

"I'm going in," said Bertie, suddenly, as Billy was crediting himself with a fifty-cent gain. "What's your score?"

"Two seventy-five, counting your break on Parmenides. It'll be cold."

"No, it won't. Well, I'm only a quarter behind you." And Bertie pulled off his shoes. Soon he splashed into the stream where the bend made a hole of some depth.

"Cold?" inquired Billy on the bank.

Bertie closed his eyes dreamily. "Delicious," said he, and sank luxuriously beneath the surface with slow strokes.

Billy had his clothes off in a moment, and, taking the plunge, screamed loudly. "You liar!" he yelled, as he came up. And he made for Bertie.

Delight rendered Bertie weak and helpless; he was caught and ducked; and after some vigorous wrestling both came out of the icy water.

"Now we've got no towels, you fool," said Billy.

"Use your notes," said Bertie, and

he rolled in the grass. Then they chased each other round the apple trees, and the black gelding watched them by the wall, its ears well forward.

While they were dressing they discovered it was half-past one, and became instantly famished. "We should have brought lunch along," they told each other. But they forgot that no such thing as lunch could have induced them to delay their escape from Cambridge for a moment this morning. "What do you suppose Oscar is doing now?" Billy inquired of Bertie, as they led the black gelding back to the road; and Bertie laughed like an infant. "Gentlemen," said he, in Oscar's manner, "we now approach the multiplicity of the ego." The black gelding must have thought it had humorists to deal with this day.

Oscar, as a matter of fact, was eating his cheap lunch away over in Cambridge. There was cold mutton, and boiled potatoes with hard brown spots in them, and large pickled cucumbers; and the salt was damp and would not shake out through the holes in the top of the bottle. But Oscar ate two helps of everything with a good appetite, and between whiles looked at his notes, which lay open beside him on the table. At the stroke of two he was again knocking at his pupils' door. But no answer came. John had gone away somewhere for indefinite hours and the door was locked. So Oscar wrote: "Called, two P.M.," on a scrap of envelope, signed his name, and put it through the letter-slit. It crossed his mind to hunt other pupils for his vacant time, but he decided against this at once, and returned to his own room. Three o'clock found him back at the door, knocking scrupulously. The idea of performing his side of the contract, of tendering his goods and standing ready at all times to deliver them, was in his commercially mature mind. This time he had brought a neat piece of paper with him, and wrote upon it, "Called, three P.M.," and signed it as before, and departed to his room with a sense of fulfilled obligations.

Bertie and Billy had lunched at Mattapan quite happily on cold ham, cold pie, and doughnuts. Mattapan, not being accustomed to such lilies of the field, stared at their clothes and general glory, but observed that they could eat the native bill-of-fare as well as anybody. They found some good, cool beer, moreover, and spoke to several people of the Bird-in-Hand, and got several answers: for instance, that the Bird-in-Hand was at Hingham; that it was at Nantasket; that they had better inquire for it at South Braintree; that they had passed it a mile back; and that there was no such place. If you would gauge the intelligence of our population, inquire your way in a rural neighborhood. With these directions they took up their journey after an hour and a half, — a halt made chiefly for the benefit of the black gelding, whom they looked after as much as they did themselves. For a while they discussed club matters seriously, as both of them were officers of certain organizations, chosen so on account of their recognized executive gifts. These questions settled, they resumed the lighter theme of philosophy, and made it (as Billy observed) a near thing for the Causal law. But as they drove along, their minds left this topic on the abrupt discovery that the sun was getting down out of the sky, and they asked each other where they were and what they should do. They pulled up at some cross-roads and debated this with growing uneasiness. Behind them lay the way to Cambridge, — not very clear, to be sure; but you could always go where you had come from, Billy seemed to think. He asked, "How about Cambridge and a little Oscar to finish off with?" Bertie frowned. This would be failure. Was Billy willing to go back and face John the successful?

"It would only cost me five dollars," said Billy.

"Ten," Bertie corrected. He recalled to Billy the matter about the landlady's hair.

"By Jove, that's so!" cried Billy, brightening. It seemed conclusive. But he grew cloudy again the next moment. He was of opinion that one could go too far in a thing.

"Where's your sand?" said Bertie.

Billy made an unseemly rejoinder, but even in the making was visited by inspiration. He saw the whole thing as it really was. "By Jove!" said he, "we couldn't get back in time for dinner."

"There's my bonny boy!" said Bertie, with pride; and he touched up the black gelding. Uneasiness had left both of them. Cambridge was manifestly impossible; an error in judgment; food compelled them to seek the Bird-in-Hand. "We'll try Quincy, anyhow," Bertie said. Billy suggested that they inquire of people on the road. This pro-

"'Come as near spillin' as you boys wanted, I guess.'"

vided a new sporting event: they could bet upon the answers. Now, the roads, not populous at noon, had grown solitary in the sweetness of the long twilight. Voices of birds there were; and little, black, quick brooks, full to the margin grass, shot under the roadway through low bridges. Through the web of young foliage the sky shone saffron, and frogs piped in the meadow swamps. No cart or carriage appeared, however, and the bets languished. Bertie, driving with one hand, was buttoning his coat with the other, when the black gelding leaped from the middle of the road to the turf and took to backing. The buggy reeled; but the driver was skilful, and fifteen seconds of whip and presence of mind brought it out smoothly. Then the cause of all this spoke to them from a gate.

"Come as near spillin' as you boys wanted, I guess," remarked the cause.

They looked, and saw him in huge white shirt-sleeves, shaking with joviality. "If you kep' at it long enough, you might a-most learn to drive a horse," he continued, eying Bertie. This came as near direct praise as the true son of our soil— Northern or Southern — often thinks well of. Bertie was pleased, but made a modest observation, and "Are we near the tavern?" he asked. "Bird-in-Hand!" the son of the soil echoed; and he contemplated them from his gate. "That's me," he stated with complacence. "Bill Diggs of the Bird-in-Hand has been me since April, '65." His massy hair had been yellow, his broad body must have weighed two hundred and fifty pounds, his wide face was canny, red, and somewhat clerical, resembling Henry Ward Beecher's.

"Trout," he said, pointing to a basket by the gate. "For your dinner." Then he climbed heavily but skilfully down and picked up the basket and a rod. "Folks round here say," said he, "that there ain't no more trout up them meadows. They've been a-sayin' that since '74; and I've been a-sayin' it myself, when judicious." Here he shook slightly and opened the basket. "Twelve," he said. "Sixteen yesterday. Now you go along and turn in the first right-hand turn, and I'll be up with you soon. Maybe you might make room for the trout." Room for him as well, they assured him; they were in luck to find him, they explained. "Well, I guess I'll trust my neck with you," he said to Bertie, the skilful driver; "'tain't five minutes' risk." The buggy leaned, and its springs bent as he climbed in, wedging his mature bulk between their slim shapes. The gelding looked round the shaft at them. "Protestin', are you?" he said to it. "These light-weight stoodents spile you!" So the gelding went on, expressing, however, by every line of its body, a sense of outraged justice. The boys related their difficult search, and learned that any mention of the name of Diggs would have brought them straight. "Bill Diggs of the Bird-in-Hand was my father, and my grandf'ther, and his father; and has been me sence I come back from the war and took the business in '65. I'm not commonly to be met out this late. About fifteen minutes earlier is my time for gettin' back, unless I'm plannin' for a jamboree. But to-night I got to settin' and watchin' that sunset, and listenin' to a darned red-winged blackbird, and I guess Mrs. Diggs has decided to expect me somewheres about noon to-morrow or Friday. Say, did Johnnie send you?" When he found that John had in a measure been responsible for their journey, he filled with gayety. "Oh, Johnnie's a bird!" said he. "He's that demure on first appearance. Walked in last evening and wanted dinner. Did he tell you what he ate? Guess he left out what he drank. Yes, he's demure."

You might suppose that upon their landlord's safe and sober return fifteen minutes late, instead of on the expected noon of Thursday or Friday, their landlady would show signs of pleasure; but Mrs. Diggs from the porch threw an uncordial eye at the three arriving in the buggy. Here were two more like Johnnie of last night. She knew them by the clothes they wore and by the confidential tones of her husband's voice as he chatted to them. He had been old enough to know better for twenty years. But for twenty years he had taken the same extreme joy in the company of Johnnies, and they were bad for his health. Her final proof that they belonged to this hated breed was when Mr. Diggs thumped the trout down on the porch, and after briefly remarking, "Half of 'em boiled, and half broiled with bacon," himself led away the gelding to the stable instead of intrusting it to his man Silas.

"You may set in the parlor," said Mrs. Diggs, and departed stiffly with the basket of trout.

"It's false," said Billy, at once.

Bertie did not grasp his thought.

"Her hair," said Billy. And certainly it was an unusual-looking arrangement.

Presently, as they sat near a parlor organ in the presence of earnest family portraits, Bertie made a new poem for Billy, —

> "Said Aristotle unto Plato,
> 'Have another sweet potato?'"

And Billy responded, —

> "Said Plato unto Aristotle,
> 'Thank you, I prefer the bottle.'"

"In here, are you?" said their beaming host at the door. "Now, I think you'd find my department of the premises cosier, so to speak." He nudged Bertie. "Do you boys guess it's too early in the season for a silver-fizz?"

We must not wholly forget Oscar in Cambridge. During the afternoon he had not failed in his punctuality; two more neat witnesses to this lay on the door-mat beneath the letter-slit of Billy's room. And at the appointed hour after dinner a third joined them, making five. John found these cards when he came home to go to bed, and picked them up and stuck them ornamentally in Billy's looking-glass, as a greeting when Billy should return. The eight o'clock visit was the last that Oscar paid to the locked door. He remained through the evening in his own room, studious, contented, unventilated, indulging in his thick notes, and also in the thought of Billy's and Bertie's eleventh-hour scholarship. "Even with another day," he told himself, "those young men could not have got fifty per cent." In those times this was the passing mark. To-day I believe you get an A, or a B, or some other letter denoting your rank. In due time Oscar turned out his gas and got into his bed; and the clocks of Massachusetts struck midnight.

Mrs. Diggs of the Bird-in-Hand had retired at eleven, furious with rage, but firm in dignity in spite of a sudden misadventure. Her hair, being the subject of a sporting event, had remained steadily fixed in Billy's mind, — steadily fixed throughout an entertainment which began at an early hour to assume the features of a celebration. One silver-fizz before dinner is nothing; but dinner did not come at once, and the boys were thirsty. The hair of Mrs. Diggs had caught Billy's eye again immediately upon her entrance to inform them that the meal was ready; and whenever she reëntered with a new course from the kitchen, Billy's eye wandered back to it, although Mr. Diggs had become full of anecdotes about the Civil War. It was partly Grecian: a knot stood out behind to a considerable distance. But this was not the whole plan. From front to back ran a parting, clear and severe, and curls fell from this to the temples in a manner called, I believe, by the enlightened, *à l'Anne d'Autriche.* The color was gray, to be sure; but this propriety did not save the structure from Billy's increasing observation. As bottles came to stand on the table in greater numbers, the closer and the more solemnly did Billy continue to follow the movements of Mrs. Diggs. They would without doubt have noticed him and his foreboding gravity but for Mr. Diggs's experiences in the Civil War.

The repast was finished — so far as eating went. Mrs. Diggs with changeless dudgeon was removing and washing the dishes. At the revellers' elbows stood the 1820 port in its fine, fat, old, dingy bottle, going pretty fast. Mr. Diggs was nearing the end of Antietam. "That morning of the 18th, while McClellan was holdin' us squattin' and cussin'," he was saying to Bertie, when some sort of shuffling sound in the corner caught their attention. We can never know how it happened. Billy ought to know, but does not, and Mrs.

Diggs allowed no subsequent reference to the casualty. But there she stood with her entire hair at right angles. The Grecian knot extended above her left ear, and her nose stuck through one set of Anne d'Autriche. Beside her Billy stood, solemn as a stone, yet with a sort of relief glazed upon his face.

Mr. Diggs sat straight up at the vision of his spouse. "Flouncing Florence!" was his exclamation. "Gee-whittaker, Mary, if you ain't the most unmitigated sight!" And wind then left him.

Mary's reply arrived in tones like a hornet stinging slowly and often. "Mr. Diggs, I have put up with many things, and am expecting to put up with many more. But you'd behave better if you consorted with gentlemen."

The door slammed and she was gone. Not a word to either of the boys, not even any notice of them. It was thorough, and silence consequently held them for a moment.

"He didn't mean anything," said Bertie, growing partially responsible.

"Didn't mean anything," repeated Billy, like a lesson.

"I'll take him and he'll apologize," Bertie pursued, walking over to Billy.

"He'll apologize," went Billy, like a cheerful piece of mechanism. Responsibility was still quite distant from him.

Mr. Diggs got his wind back. "Better not," he advised in something near a whisper. "Better not go after her. Her father was a fightin' preacher, and she's — well, begosh! she's a chip of the old pulpit." And he rolled his eye towards the door. Another door slammed somewhere above, and they gazed at each other, did Bertie and Mr. Diggs. Then Mr. Diggs, still gazing at Bertie, beckoned to him with a speaking eye and a crooked finger; and as he beckoned, Bertie approached like a conspirator and sat down close to him. "Begosh!" whispered Mr. Diggs. "Unmitigated." And at this he and

Bertie laid their heads down on the table and rolled about in spasms.

Billy from his corner seemed to become aware of them. With his eye fixed upon them like a statue, he came across the room, and, sitting down near them with formal politeness, observed, "Was you ever to the battle of Antietam?" This sent them beyond the limit; and they rocked their heads on the table and wept as if they would expire.

Thus the three remained, during what space of time is not known: the two upon the table, convalescent with relapses, and Billy like a seated idol, unrelaxed at his vigil. The party was seen through the windows by Silas, coming from the stable to inquire if the gelding should not be harnessed. Silas leaned his face to the pane, and envy spoke plainly in it. "O my! O my!" he mentioned aloud to himself. So we have the whole household: Mrs. Diggs reposing scornfully in an upper chamber; all parts of the tavern darkened, save the one lighted room; the three inside that among their bottles, with the one outside looking covetously in at them; and the gelding stamping in the stable.

But Silas, since he could not share, was presently of opinion that this was enough for one sitting, and he tramped heavily upon the porch. This brought Bertie back to the world of reality, and word was given to fetch the gelding. The host was in no mood to part with them, and spoke of comfortable beds and breakfast as early as they liked; but Bertie had become entirely responsible. Billy was helped in, Silas was liberally thanked, and they drove away beneath the stars, leaving behind them golden opinions, and a host who decided not to disturb his helpmate by retiring to rest in their conjugal bed.

Bertie had forgotten, but the playful gelding had not. When they came abreast of that gate where Diggs of the

Bird-in-Hand had met them at sunset, Bertie was only aware that a number of things had happened at once, and that he had stopped the horse after about twenty yards of battle. Pride filled him, but emptied away in the same instant, for a voice on the road behind him spoke inquiringly through the darkness.

"Did any one fall out?" said the voice. "Who fell out?"

"Billy!" shrieked Bertie, cold all over. "Billy, are you hurt?"

"Did Billy fall out?" said the voice, with plaintive cadence. "Poor Billy!"

"He can't be," muttered Bertie. "Are you?" he loudly repeated.

There was no answer; but steps came along the road as Bertie checked and pacified the gelding. Then Billy appeared by the wheel. "Poor Billy fell out," he said mildly. He held something up, which Bertie took. It had been Billy's straw hat, now a brimless fabric of ruin. Except for smirches and one inexpressible rent which dawn revealed to Bertie a little later, there were no further injuries, and Billy got in and took his seat quite competently.

Bertie drove the geiding with a firm hand after this. They passed through the cool of the unseen meadow swamps, and heard the sound of the hollow bridges as they crossed them, and now and then the gulp of some pouring brook. They went by the few lights of Mattapan, seeing from some points on their way the beacons of the harbor, and again the curving line of lamps that drew the outline of some village built upon a hill. Dawn showed them Jamaica Pond, smooth and breezeless, and encircled with green skeins of foliage, delicate and new. Here multitudinous birds were chirping their tiny, overwhelming chorus. When at length, across the flat suburban spaces, they again sighted Memorial tower, small in the distance, the sun was lighting it.

Confronted by this, thoughts of hitherto banished care, and of the morrow that was now to-day, and of Philosophy 4 coming in a very few hours, might naturally have arisen and darkened the end of their pleasant excursion. Not so, however. Memorial tower suggested another line of argument. It was Billy who spoke, as his eyes first rested upon that eminent pinnacle of Academe.

"Well, John owes me five dollars."

"Ten, you mean."

"Ten? How?"

"Why, her hair. And it was easily worth twenty."

Billy turned his head and looked suspiciously at Bertie. "What did I do?" he asked.

"Do! Don't you know?"

Billy in all truth did not.

"Phew!" went Bertie. "Well, I don't, either. Didn't see it. Saw the consequences, though. Don't you remember being ready to apologize? What do you remember, anyhow?"

Billy consulted his recollections with care: they seemed to break off at the champagne. That was early. Bertie was astonished. Did not Billy remember singing "Brace up and dress the Countess," and "A noble lord the Earl of Leicester"? He had sung them quite in his usual manner, conversing freely between whiles. In fact, to see and hear him, no one would have suspected— "It must have been that extra silver-fizz you took before dinner," said Bertie. "Yes," said Billy; "that's what it must have been." Bertie supplied the gap in his memory,— a matter of several hours, it seemed. During most of this time Billy had met the demands of each moment quite like his usual agreeable self—a sleep-walking state. It was only when the hair incident was reached that his conduct had noticeably crossed the line. He listened to all this with interest intense.

"John does owe me ten, I think," said he.

"I say so," declared Bertie. "When do you begin to remember again?"

"After I got in again at the gate. Why did I get out?"

"You fell out, man."

Billy was incredulous.

"You did. You tore your clothes wide open."

Billy, looking at his trousers, did not see it.

"Rise, and I'll show you," said Bertie.

"Goodness gracious!" said Billy.

Thus discoursing, they reached Harvard Square. Not your Harvard Square, gentle reader, that place populous with careless youths and careful maidens and reticent persons with books, but one of sleeping windows and clear, cool air and few sounds; a Harvard Square of emptiness and conspicuous sparrows and milk wagons and early street-car conductors in long coats going to their breakfast; and over all this the sweetness of the arching elms.

As the gelding turned down toward Pike's, the thin old church clock struck.

"Always sounds," said Billy, "like cambric tea."

"Cambridge tea," said Bertie.

"Walk close behind me," said Billy, as they came away from the livery stable. "Then they won't see the hole."

Bertie did so; but the hole was seen by the street-car conductors and the milkmen, and these sympathetic hearts smiled at the sight of the marching boys, and loved them without knowing any more of them than this. They reached their building and separated.

V

V

ONE hour later they met. Shaving and a cold bath and summer flannels, not only clean but beautiful, invested them with the radiant innocence of flowers. It was still too early for their regular breakfast, and they sat down to eggs and coffee at the Holly Tree.

"I waked John up," said Billy. "He is satisfied."

"Let's have another order," said Bertie. "These eggs are delicious." Each of them accordingly ate four eggs and drank two cups of coffee.

"Oscar called five times," said Billy; and he threw down those cards which Oscar had so neatly written.

"There's multiplicity of the ego for you!" said Bertie.

Now, inspiration is a strange thing, and less obedient even than love to the will of man. It will decline to come when you prepare for it with the loftiest intentions, and, lo! at an accidental word it will suddenly fill you, as at this moment it filled Billy.

"By gum!" said he, laying his fork down. "Multiplicity of the ego. Look here. I fall out of a buggy and ask —"

"By gum!" said Bertie, now also visited by inspiration.

"Don't you see?" said Billy.

"I see a whole lot more," said Bertie, with excitement. "I had to tell you about your singing." And the two burst into a flare of talk.

To hear such words as cognition, attention, retention, entity, and identity, freely mingled with such other words as silver-fizz and false hair, brought John, the egg-and-coffee man, as near surprise as his impregnable nature permitted. Thus they finished their large breakfast, and hastened to their notes for a last good bout at memorizing Epicharmos of Kos and his various brethren. The appointed hour found them crossing the college yard toward a door inside which Philosophy 4 awaited them: three hours of written examination! But they looked more roseate and healthy than most of the anxious band whose steps were converging to that same gate of judgment. Oscar, meeting them on the way, gave them his deferential "Good morning," and trusted that the gentlemen felt easy. Quite so, they told him, and bade him feel easy about his pay, for which they were, of course, responsible. Oscar wished them good luck and watched them go to their desks with his little eyes, smiling in his particular manner. Then he dismissed them from his mind, and sat with a faint remnant of his smile, fluently writing his perfectly accurate answer to the first question upon the examination paper.

Here is that paper. You will not be able to answer all the questions, probably, but you may be glad to know what such things are like.

PHILOSOPHY 4

1. Thales, Zeno, Parmenides, Heracleitos, Anaxagoras. State briefly the doctrine of each.

2. Phenomenon, noumenon. Discuss these terms. Name their modern descendants.

3. Thought=Being. Assuming this, state the difference, if any, between (1) memory and anticipation; (2) sleep and waking.

4. Democritus, Pythagoras, Bacon. State the relation between them. In what terms must the objective world ultimately be stated? Why?

5. Experience is the result of time and space being included in the nature of mind. Discuss this.

6. Nihil est in intellectu quod non prius fuerit in sensibus. Whose doctrine? Discuss it.

7. What is the inherent limitation in all ancient philosophy? Who first removed it?

8. Mind is expressed through what? Mat-

ter through what? Is speech the result or the cause of thought?

9. Discuss the nature of the ego.

10. According to Plato, Locke, Berkeley, where would the sweetness of a honeycomb reside? Where would its shape? its weight? Where do you think these properties reside?

Ten questions, and no Epicharmos of Kos. But no examination paper asks everything, and this one did ask a good deal. Bertie and Billy wrote the full time allotted, and found that they could have filled an hour more without coming to the end of their thoughts. Comparing notes at lunch, their information was discovered to have been lacking here and there. Nevertheless, it was no failure; their inner convictions were sure of fifty per cent at least, and this was all they asked of the gods. "I was ripping about the ego," said Bertie. "I was rather splendid myself," said Billy, "when I got going. And I gave him a huge steer about memory." After lunch both retired to their beds and fell into sweet oblivion until seven o'clock, when they rose and dined, and after playing a little poker went to bed again pretty early.

Some six mornings later, when the Professor returned their papers to them, their minds were washed almost as clear of Plato and Thales as were their bodies of yesterday's dust. The dates and doctrines, hastily memorized to rattle off upon the great occasion, lay only upon the surface of their minds, and after use they quickly evaporated. To their pleasure and most genuine astonishment, the Professor paid them high compliments. Bertie's discussion of the double personality had been the most intelligent which had come in from any of the class. The illustration of the intoxicated hack-driver who had fallen from his hack and inquired who it was that had fallen, and then had pitied himself, was, said the Professor, as original and perfect an illustration of our subjective-objectivity as he had met with in all his researches. And Billy's suggestions concerning the inherency of time and space in the mind the Professor had also found very striking and independent, particularly his reasoning based upon the well-known distortions of time and space which hashish and other drugs produce in us. This was the sort of thing which the Professor had wanted from his students: free comment and discussions, the *spirit* of the course, rather than any strict adherence to the letter. He had constructed his questions to elicit as much individual discussion as possible and had been somewhat disappointed in his hopes.

Yes, Bertie and Billy were astonished. But their astonishment did not equal that of Oscar, who had answered many of the questions in the Professor's own language. Oscar received seventy-five per cent for this achievement — a good mark. But Billy's mark was eighty-six and Bertie's ninety. "There is some mistake," said Oscar to them when they told him; and he hastened to the Professor with his tale. "There is no mistake," said the Professor. Oscar smiled with increased deference. "But," he urged, "I assure you, sir, those young men knew absolutely nothing. I was their tutor, and they knew nothing at all. I taught them all their information myself." "In that case," replied the Professor, not pleased with Oscar's talebearing, "you must have given them more than you could spare. Good morning."

Oscar never understood. But he graduated considerably higher than Bertie and Billy, who were not able to discover many other courses so favorable to "orriginal rresearch" as was Philosophy 4. That is twenty years ago. To-day Bertie is treasurer of the New Amsterdam Trust Company, in Wall Street; Billy is superintendent of passenger traffic of the New York and Chicago Air Line. Oscar is successful too. He has acquired a lot of information. His smile is unchanged. He has published a careful work entitled "The Minor Poets of Cinquecento," and he writes book reviews for the *Evening Post*.

OWEN WISTER was born in Philadelphia, July 14, 1860. He is the fourth generation of his family in direct descent that has occupied itself with literature, both prose and verse. Among his forbears were members of the famous Kemble family of actors, to which belonged Mrs. Siddons, and her gifted nieces Adelaide Kemble (Mrs. Sartoris, singer, and author of "A Week in a French Country House") and Fanny Kemble, actress and writer, who was Mr. Wister's grandmother.

In 1892 he abandoned his chosen profession, the law, and began to devote himself steadily to imaginative writing, which had already for some years previous to this occupied him from time to time. His first literary production was entitled "Down in a Diving Bell," and was published in the boys' paper at St. Paul's School, when he was thirteen years old. His first contribution to a standard magazine appeared in the *Atlantic Monthly* when he was twenty-one, before his graduation from Harvard, and was a poem addressed to Beethoven. His latest published writing is a story entitled "How the Energy was Conserved," in *Collier's Weekly*, February 21, 1903. Mr. Wister's published volumes are: "The Dragon of Wantley," 1892; "Red Men and White," 1895; "Lin McLean," 1897; "Ulysses S. Grant," 1900; "The Jimmyjohn Boss," 1900; "The Virginian," 1902.

The reception of his latest book has been increasingly enthusiastic. The *Nation* says: —

> "The dramatic thrill in it is very quick, and the outcome so satisfactory that one realizes an immense fear of disappointment. 'The Virginian' is one of the most popular books of the season; it deserves to endure through many seasons."

A large part of the appeal which his books make lies in their absolute truth to the life which he studied so thoroughly, making fifteen separate journeys to the Western country within ten years. As all the critics say of his nameless hero: —

> "'The Virginian' is a 'sure-enough' man."

Mr. Hamblen Sears, reviewing "The Virginian" at length in the *The Book Buyer*, says that this is

> "fiction of the sort we want. It tells us of the real man of America in such a human, such an accurate way that we keep on saying, 'I've seen that a dozen times,' when not one of us would ever know he had seen it unless a Wister had set it down."

But almost equally strong is the charm of their perfect wholesomeness; along with the heartache of wide spaces, it is true, comes the grim tragedy of primitive life before the law reached the plains, but through it all is felt the sweep of Western winds, and sunny, exhilarating fresh air which, so the *Boston Transcript* declares,

> "ought to help the consumptive nearly as much as to breathe the real air of the real country."

> "To read this book is an unalloyed delight. It carries you along with a rush and a sweep, and at the final page you lay it down feeling full of the best brand of Western ozone, and almost sunburnt from perusing it." — *New York Sun*.

> "It is in humor — spontaneous, genuine, contagious humor — that the book especially excels. Passages that provoke hearty laughter are many, but that is a detail beside the main point, that

> this humor is of the essence of American life, that it springs naturally from the situation, and because it is the real thing it is funny as often as you come across it." — *Boston Herald*.

Yet there is far more to the book than jest or tragedy, or even its convincing picturesqueness, and pride of youth and strength.

> " It is a love story which constitutes its burden, but it is the quaintest love-making — exquisite in its humanity, its insight, its humor, its fidelity to truth." — *Brooklyn Eagle*.

> " It is a very human, very tantalizing love story." — *Boston Transcript*.

In England, as in his own country, " The Virginian " has proved " very human, very satisfying." The well-known critic, Mr. W. D. Courtney, made it the text for a long and remarkably appreciative article on the recent advance in American fiction. And " it is books like Mr. Wister's that make the true American," says the *Chicago Tribune*.

> " It is one of the best romances of the West in American literature, and by far the most striking picture of a genuine cowboy that has yet been painted." — *San Francisco Chronicle*.

BY THE SAME AUTHOR

THE VIRGINIAN

A Horseman of the Plains

By OWEN WISTER

Author of "Lin McLean," "U. S. Grant: a Biography," etc.

With eight full-page illustrations by ARTHUR I. KELLER

| Cloth | 12mo | $1.50 |

"There is not a page in Mr. Wister's new book which is not interesting. This is its first great merit, that it arouses the sympathy of the reader and holds him absorbed and amused to the end. It does a great deal more for him. . . . Whoever reads the first page will find it next to impossible to put the book down until he has read every one of the five hundred and four in the book, and then he will wish there were more of them."
— *The New York Tribune.*

"Mr. Wister has drawn real men and real women, and a day that America has centuries of reason for pride in, now passing away forever. . . . No one writes of the frontier with more interest than this young Philadelphia author, and no one writes literature more essentially American. In *The Virginian* he has put forth a book that will be remembered and read with interest for many years hence. May he soon write another as good!"
— *The Chicago American.*

THE MACMILLAN COMPANY

66 Fifth Avenue, New York

The Macmillan Little Novels

BY FAVOURITE AUTHORS

Handsomely Bound in Decorated Cloth
16mo   50 cents each

MAN OVERBOARD
By F. Marion Crawford
Author of "Cecilia," "Marietta," etc.

MR. KEEGAN'S ELOPEMENT
By Winston Churchill
Author of "The Crisis," "Richard Carvel," etc.

MRS. PENDLETON'S FOUR=IN=HAND
By Gertrude Atherton
Author of "The Conqueror," "The Splendid Idle Forties," etc.

THE MACMILLAN COMPANY
66 Fifth Avenue, New York